Jane Yolen

Welcome to the
GREEN HOUSE

Illustrated by Laura Regan

G. P. Putnam's Sons · New York

Text copyright © 1993 by Jane Yolen
Illustrations copyright © 1993 by Laura Regan
G. P. Putnam's Sons, a division of The Putnam & Grosset Group,
200 Madison Avenue, New York, NY 10016.
Published simultaneously in Canada.
Printed in Hong Kong by South China Printing Co. (1988) Ltd
Book design by Nanette Stevenson
The text is set in Meridien Medium.

Library of Congress Cataloging-in-Publication Data
Yolen, Jane.
Welcome to the green house : a story of the tropical rainforest /
Jane Yolen ; illustrated by Laura Regan.   p.   cm.
Summary: Describes the tropical rainforest and the life found there.
1. Rain forest ecology—Juvenile literature. 2. Rain forests—
Juvenile literature. [1. Rain forests. 2. Rain forest ecology.
3. Ecology.] I. Regan, Laura, ill. II. Title.
QH541.5.R27Y65 1993   574.5'2642'0913—dc20   91-22081   CIP   AC
ISBN 0-399-22335-5

10 9 8 7 6 5 4 3

To Pam Roberts and Earth Island Institute
for their ongoing efforts
to preserve the rainforest.—J.Y.

For my daughters Andrea, Elyse and Amy,
who are my finest critics
and constant source of inspiration.—L.R.

''The land is one great wild, untidy luxuriant
hothouse, made by nature for herself.''
—Charles Darwin, *Voyage of the Beagle*

Welcome to the green house.
Welcome to the hot house.
Welcome to the land of the warm, wet days.
There are no doors in the green house,
yet strong lianas bar the way.
There are no windows in the green house,
yet ropey vines frame the views.
There are no wooden floors in the green house,
only fallen leaves,
and white rootlets,
and fungal threads.
There are no walls in the green house,
only the giant forest trees.

There is no roof in the green house,
only the canopy of leaves,
where the sun and rain
poke through narrow slots;

where the slow, green-coated sloth

and the quick-fingered capuchin
make their slow-quick ways
from room to room
in the green house,
in the dark green,
light green,
emerald green,
bright green,
copper green,
blue green,
ever-new green house.

But it is not all green
in the hot green house:
a flash of blue hummingbird,
a splash of golden toad,

a lunge of waking lizards,
a plunge of silver fish,

a slide of coral snake through leaves,
a glide of butterflies through air,
past crimson flowers,
past showy orchid bowers.
Everywhere color threads through,
spreads through the hot green house.

And this is not a quiet house,
not in the day:

with the *a-hoo, a-hoo, a-hoo*
of the howler troop
welcoming the dawn;
with the *crinch-crunch*
of long-horned beetles
chewing through wood;
with the *pick-buzz-hum-buzz*
of a thousand thousand bees
droning over flowers;

with the high *chitter-chitter-rrrrr*
of the golden lion tamarin
warning off intruders;
with the *kre-ek, kre-ek, kre-ek*
of keel-billed toucans
feeding on ripe, sweet figs;
with the *sniff-sniff-sniff*
beneath the fig tree
where the wild pig picks
through the fallen fruit.

This is not a quiet house,
not even in the night:

with the *chirr-chirrup*
of chorusing frogs
from limbs and logs,
from trunks and leaves,
from the water's edge,
from the rocky ledge,
welcoming the dark;

with the *kwah-kwa-kwa-kwo*
of the boat-billed herons
fishing in the river;
with the *whup-whup-whoosh*
of the fluttering bats
flying through the evening air;
with the *twitter-ee, twitter-ees*
of the kinkajous
calling from the tops of trees,

alert for the soft *grrrrrrrroooooowl*
of the ocelot
on the prowl
for its next meal.

This is a loud house.
A bright house.
A day house.
A night house.
A wet house.
A warm house.
A single and
A swarm house.
A monkey house.
A tree house.
A fish and bird and
bee house.

Welcome to the green house
and the hot summer days.

Did You Know?

Tropical rainforests cover only six percent of our Earth, but they are home to two thirds of all the species of plants and animals in our world. You would think that we would be taking very good care of this green house.

However, in the last hundred years, we have cut down over half the world's rainforests. Today we are destroying fifty acres a minute. Every minute.

If we do not do something soon, there will be no more green house, not for the monkeys and fish and birds and bees and beetles and wild pigs and bats and kinkajous and all the hundreds of thousands of flowers and fruits and trees. And not for us either.

If you are interested in learning more about the rainforest and ways to preserve it, get in touch with

Earth Island Institute
300 Broadway, Suite 28
San Francisco
CA 94133